THE DIARY OF MARJORIE EGGHEAD

Dedicated to the original Marjorie

Illustrated by Lucia Garwood-Gowers

Friday

Yes! Today was my final day of Year 6 at John Wood Primary School. I've been going there since I was four years old so I suppose it was quite a sad day. But I have to say, it's a massive relief more than anything else. The whole time there - 7 years - I have managed to keep a very big secret. Ruby, my best friend is the only person that knows and is sworn to absolute secrecy. If it had ever got out, I would have been finished! My secret: 'Marjorie Egghead' - my awful nickname.

I honestly don't think there is another name on this planet that is quite as bad.

It was invented by David – my revolting big brother - who I truly believe to be the worst brother on this planet!

So, how did he come up with this hideous name? Marjorie is my middle name - I was named after my Great Grandma. Back in the day, Marjorie may have been a popular name, but in the 21st century it's a big, NO!

The 'Egghead' bit is unfortunately not because I am highly intelligent - although I'm not totally stupid either - it's because, not only did I inherit Marjorie's name, but I inherited her huge forehead too - how unlucky is that! I've tried loads of tricks over the years to get my fringe to cover my massive forehead, but it just pings up - 'the egg' in full view.

So, like I said, I somehow managed to get through primary school without anyone finding out. But now I must start all over again when I begin secondary school in 6 weeks - another 5 years of trying to keep my secret! The good news is though - David won't be there! Today was his last day at secondary school.

He reckons his teachers think he's charming and will be sad to see him go, but I have my doubts.

I'm pretty sure he would have been horrid to his teachers because he sure is a horrid brother and he has tormented me for as long as I can remember. His greeting to me has always been the same.

Mom and Dad's advice - 'Just ignore him, and he will stop doing it.' But no matter how much I try, I'm not quite there yet.

As well as the maker of my mean nickname, he has carried out many other wicked deeds over the years like: throwing my teddies out the window,

tricking me into eating one of his bogeys,

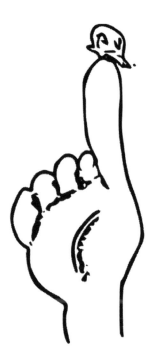

throwing a dart into my bum,

forcing me to play Monopoly for hours even though I'm bankrupt after 20 minutes,

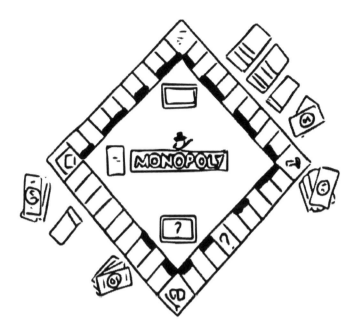

and probably the worst of them all - the 'Gob drop' treatment.

I've experienced this many times and it is truly horrific. David pins my arms down, sits on me so I can't move, and then collects a load of gob in his mouth and slowly lowers it down - aiming for my face! At the last minute he sucks it back up and starts all over again.

Once though, he lost control and I ended up with a huge dollop of his gob on my cheek. I know, he is truly disgusting! All these things are very well timed, so Mom and Dad never get to see it. So, I think you'll agree, no matter how bad you think your brother is, mine is worse!

My younger sister Emily isn't quite as bad but can still be an absolute pain! Having to share a room with her has zero advantages but loads of disadvantages. She borrows my things and breaks them, wakes me up if she gets scared in the night, and I even have to go to bed at the same time as her - 7pm - just so she'll go to sleep.

The worst thing of all though, is her wall of bogies! Yes, Emily has the most disgusting habit ever - she wipes her bogies on the wall next to her bed!

I mean why can't she just eat them like most kids! I've had nightmares about the bogey wall for years. At night when everyone is asleep, the bogeys come to life! They pull themselves off the wall, crawl along her bed, and slither across the floor up to me! So many times I've woken suddenly in the night in a panic, checking myself over for her gross bogeys.

Mom and Dad tried to scrape them off once, but the damage was already done - they were set on the wall like concrete! So they painted over them instead to try and get them to blend in with the wood chip wallpaper. And now, every 6 months or so, the paint comes out and another layer is put on top of the bogeys!

Another thing that bugs me about Emily, is that she never gets into trouble. I would say, without doubt, she is the favourite in the family. All she has to do is shed a few tears and Mom and Dad give into her every time.

At the end of school today though, I thought she may have pushed her luck a little too far. She was waiting by the school gate for me with a massive grin on her face, holding a cage, and inside was Hercules the school hamster! I was convinced Mom and Dad were going to flip! Mom is scared of anything small and fury and Dad is one of those people that thinks animals should not be allowed in the house.
I so wanted Emily to get into trouble so I told her it was a great idea!

Mom and Dad will be delighted!

As soon as we got home, Mom's reaction did not disappoint. She frantically tried to call the school to get them to take it back. But who was she kidding? It was now 4' o' clock - half an hour since school finished. The teachers would be long gone.

So, the usual order of events took place. Emily turned on the tears and Mom and Dad changed their minds! It happens every time - they are such pushovers - especially Dad!

As well as being pushovers I would have to add naive and gullible to the list too.

When David arrived home from his last day at school, I had to sit and watch Mom and Dad being reeled in by him yet again. Firstly, they were actually admiring his graffitied shirt - an end of year 11 tradition. They seemed to miss the obscenities and just commented on what lovely colours had been used. The only thing that seemed to annoy Dad was some of the spelling mistakes.

When he handed Mom his *Year Book* though, I was certain he would be in for it. A Year Book is what you get when you leave seconday school, and it has everyone's photo from year 11 with a quote written by fellow students about how that person will be best remembered. His quote was sure to be something to do with him being an absolute pain over the last 5 years. Mom opened the book and as I waited for her to start chewing the inside of her cheek – a sign she is really cross - a huge smile spread across her face instead. David's quote was, 'Will be best remembered for the most Field Runs.' I stood in disbelief as Mom and Dad jumped up and down with excitement and started congratulating him! They thought it meant he had the record for some kind of athletic event! They had no idea what 'Field runs' were, but I knew exactly what they were!

 Ruby – best friend - has an older sister in the same year as David and she is always telling me the gossip about him. David has no athletic record whatsoever! His so called record of 'Most Field runs' is for an illegal event that happens during break times. When the school field is too wet and out of bounds, it's a chance for the year 11 boys to wind up the teachers. They walk outside for break as normal, then one of the boys will shout, 'Field Run!' All those brave enough to run around the out of bounds field, go for it, while the teachers on duty attempt to chase after them.

It sounds quite funny, but it made me so mad listening to Mom and Dad gushing about how their son is the year 11 athletics champion! I was about to explain to them what it really means, when I glanced across at my horrid brother. He silently mouthed, 'Gob drop' to me and I quickly changed my mind. The good news is though, in 6 months time he is leaving home to join the Army! What a celebration that is going to be for me!

So, after all the drama of Hercules the hamster and the 'Field run champion,' I thought I would try and get a bit of attention myself. I reminded Mom and Dad that it's my birthday in a few months – I like to be prepared - and I wanted to think about who I'll invite and where we can go, but Dad made a quick exit and Mom said she was too tired to talk birthdays - it would have to wait. Seriously!

I've come to the opinion that parents only have a certain amount of attention they can dish out. And in our house, the youngest gets the first offerings, then the eldest. So, if you're in the middle - like me - you pretty much get the dregs.

10	EXTRAORDINARY
9	OUTSTANDING
8	FAR-REACHING
7	HIGH
6	NOTEWORTHY
5	INTERMEDIATE
4	MODERATE
3	MINOR
2	LOW
1	INSIGNIFICANT
0	NONE

Saturday

Well, after last night I'm pretty furious. It seems Hercules is a hyperactive hamster! For the whole night, he was either on his wheel - going round like a crazy thing - or biting his cage trying to get out. He obviously has some kind of cage rage problem!

I barely got any sleep, but Emily slept through the whole thing! At 6am he'd finally run out of energy and went to sleep. I decided to ban Hercules from my room, but Mom managed to persuade me to try one more night as she had a plan. She bought him an exercise ball and she convinced me that a few hours racing around the house in this plastic ball, would make him so tired that he would sleep through the night.

So, after dinner we put him in his new ball and off he went! It was hilarious watching him racing around like a mini speed machine. Poor Charlie our cat wasn't too happy though.

What we didn't notice with all this entertainment going on, was Hercules had - shall we say - relieved himself. I suppose hamsters are no different to humans - when you gotta go - you gotta go. Luckily, humans usually make it to the toilet rather than doing it right there, right then.

Well, what happened next has, without doubt, ensured that Emily won't ever be getting her own pet hamster.

Dad walked into the sitting room to see what we were all laughing at. He was soon laughing with the rest of us - especially as Hercules was scaring the life out of poor Charlie. Dad has never liked Charlie – the feeling is mutual though. Anyway, I caught Dad out the corner of my eye as he bent down – still laughing - and picked up the 'raisins.' Emily always drops her raisins on the floor when she tries to empty the whole box into her mouth. Let me tell you – hamster poo is identical to raisins! I realised too late to warn poor Dad. Time seemed to stand still as I watched him empty the whole pile into his mouth!

Well, he must have some kind of time delay to his taste buds, as it took at least 10 chomps before they were spewed back out with the loudest shriek I have ever heard.

'They aren't raisins Dad!' came too late from me. We all acted with genuine concern to start off with. But not for long. Mom was first to crack, and then we were all doubled over laughing at Dad's rotten luck. Charlie looked especially pleased - his number one enemy had just eaten poo!

I'm so happy!

Understandably, Dad was pretty annoyed – in fact so annoyed that his pop-up vein appeared. This is a vein on the side of his forehead which gets bigger whenever he's cross, and Dad's vein looked like it was going to explode! My delight at Dad's misfortune didn't last though, because Hercules' punishment was being grounded for the rest of the summer - to my bedroom! Well, isn't that just tickety-boo!!

Monday

So last night, I thought the exercise ball must have done the trick as I didn't hear a peep out of him. But when I woke up, I noticed the cage door was open – the rascal had escaped! It might sound ridiculous, but I'm wondering if he over-heard Dad saying that he was grounded.

We spent most of the day searching for him, but he was nowhere to be found. Then we had to listen to Emily cry for most of the day. Well at least we have 6 weeks to try and find him!

Wednesday

Still no sign of Hecules and things seem to be going from bad to worse. Today I accidentally ran through the GLASS door in the lounge. As usual, it was totally David's fault, but I've ended up in trouble too. Mom had decided we were having a no-electronics day. Without his phone or X-box, David has no way to entertain himself, so just for fun, he pulled all the heads off my dolls! I was fuming and chased him round the house in a complete rage. I pushed the lounge door pretty hard when he shut it on me, and I ended up going straight through it! Mom and Dad were out at the time, so I thought about blaming it on Charlie, but the evidence was pretty conclusive, and now I have to use my pocket money to get it fixed! So unfair!

Thursday

The tension in the house definitely seems to be building day by day. Today, Dad found sucker marks on the TV! David had apparently been practising his shot with Emily's toy bow and arrow. Dad was not happy as it's a brand-new TV - Dad's pride and joy.

He tried to argue with Dad that it was for his army training, but I don't think Dad was buying it.

Friday

Today I pulled off a master plan and I still can't quite believe it! Emily is moving out of my room! With 3 kids and 3 bedrooms - one room being for Mom and Dad - I'm not sure where they are going to put her but hey - not my problem! Let me explain how I pulled it off.

Mom decided in the morning, without any warning, to send us all to a sports camp. Not sure why, but she does seem pretty stressed having us all at home. Mom claimed the sports camp was to keep us fit and healthy, but I'm guessing she just wants us out the house. Me and David are too old for the camp – me by 1 year, but David by 5 years! So she offered to pay us if we lied about our age. I agreed to lie without any payment, if she moved Emily out of my bedroom. She agreed!

Saying I was 10 when I'm actually only 1 year older was pretty easy, but when it came to David's turn to lie about his age, it was just a little obvious. He is 16 and nearly as tall as Dad!

I think they must have felt awkward about turning him away because they let him stay. But what's worse, he was quite happy to go along with it - does he have no self-respect? He was having to spend the whole day with a bunch of primary school kids! What a loser! He did get Mom to pay him £50 though, so maybe it's Mom who's the loser!

As the day went on, I became more and more embarrassed with my moron of a brother. He basically won every single medal that was on offer. From the hurdles to the sprint, and the high jump to the javelin. So many kids left in tears and David was genuinely delighted that he had beaten a bunch of kids that were half his age! When Mom picked us up, she tried to book us in for next week, but apparently they were full!

Saturday

I reminded Mom about the agreement we made yesterday, but she started chewing the inside of her cheek and I knew it would have to wait. I think she is panicking that she has nowhere to send us next week.

I can already feel boredom setting in and it's only the end of the first week. I can't meet up with Ruby as she is away for the whole of the 6 weeks. Can you believe it -she is going around Europe in a camper van with her parents and sister. Sounds great, but the thought of having to share a confined space with any member of my family does not sound like a holiday! We are meant to be moving house soon, so no family holiday this year. Apparently - according to Mom and Dad - there is lots to do when you move house. Surely it can't be that much effort packing up a few boxes - parents really do exaggerate at times!

I don't really want to move, but Mom can't wait. She has had it in for the people that live in the retirement flats next to us from day 1, and we have lived here for 8 years. It's because whenever David, Emily and me are in the garden, it normally ends up being some kind of squabbling or brawling match.

I've often noticed, when we are in full flow, several pairs of eyes staring down at us from the flats. To be fair, it must be quite entertaining but I think Mom is a bit paranoid as she thinks they are judging her parenting skills. Sometimes, I can't say I can blame them.

24

Sunday

Well, if we weren't already moving, we are now after what happened this morning. Normally, Mom is really calm, but whenever we are on school holidays, she gets stressed.

Kids at school

Kids at home

I would say today, her stress levels hit an all-time high. I knew something was wrong when she said she was going out for a run – Mom is normally the gentle stroll type. Well, about an hour later I could hear Mom yelling at the top of her voice and it was coming from outside. I looked out the window and there she was, bent down and shouting - through our next-door neighbour's letterbox!

The yelling and banging continued for a couple of minutes, and I suppose I should have shouted out to her and asked what she was doing, but I was pretty keen to see the expression on her face when she realised she was at the wrong house. Let's just say it did not disappoint! All the noise had alerted pretty much everyone in the whole street! It really was a great scene, and I think the people in the retirement home couldn't quite believe their luck!

Ben - our next-door neighbour - opened the door - wearing his boxer shorts! I'm guessing Mom was unable to speak when she realised her mistake. She was in so much shock, she stood frozen for a few seconds and then fled with her mouth aghast looking like she was about to pass out.

Monday

The ordeal of yesterday and the whole week, has obviously tipped Mom over the edge, as I can't believe what I've just read. Okay, I know I shouldn't have, but I read her diary when I went into her room. It read, 'The kids are driving me mad. I can't cope having them around for another day, let alone another 5 weeks. I'm going to have to send them to their Grandad's for a week.'

This is going to be a bit weird as Mom hasn't spoken to Grandad for nearly a year! Mom fell out with him when she left him in charge of looking after Charlie. Mom loves Charlie; I think sometimes even more than any of us! Anyway, we were away for a few days and Grandad was in charge. Pretty simple instructions: feed twice a day and let him in and out to poop. I'll never forget the conversation when Grandad picked us up from the train station, 'And how has Charlie been Dad?' Mom asked.

'Well how should I know how Charlie has been?' Grandad realised as soon as the last word came out of his mouth.

Ooops..sorry I forgot!

I think we were all expecting a half-dead Charlie when we got back to the house. Five days without food or water!
I can't be sure, but when we opened the front door, Dad looked slightly disappointed to see Charlie sitting at the top of the stairs - alive and well.
I can't be sure again, but I'm certain I saw Charlie give dad a wink as they locked eyes.

I'm still here and still No.1

Anyway, Mom must be desperate to get rid of us. Grandad is obviously not trustworthy to look after a cat, but she is more than happy for him to look after us! Surely, we can't be that bad! I'm still hoping I can make her change

29

her mind. It will be so boring - Grandad's Wi-Fi signal is rubbish - what on earth will I do? I told David and Emily of Mom's plan and they started panicking too. We would have to join forces to get her to change her mind.

So, for the rest of the day none of us argued, which I have to say was pretty tough going. David attempted to charm Mom and Dad, but I would say he definitely needs to work on it.

But later in the evening, they broke the news - we are leaving tomorrow! And the worse of it is that they are making it a 'digital detox week' – A DOUBLE DISASTER!! I totally blame David for the digital detox bit. Mom and Dad have been threatening this for a while - last month, David got so carried away with a stupid on-line game, he ended up buying 14,000 virtual gems for £125.

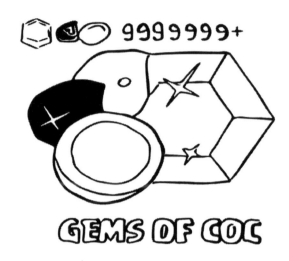

Of course, it was all linked to Mom and Dad's account - and they were not happy! And it's always David who will never come off the X-box. 'In a minute - if I come off now I'll die!' is the most said phrase in our house.

I promised Mom I would limit my time on my phone and be more helpful, if I could stay at home, but she said she needs us out of the house anyway so she can pack for the house move. Now, we have only just sold our house and I'm pretty sure it takes a while before you actually move, so Mom is either being super organised or just trying to get rid of us! Surprise, surprise though with Emily. She cried, and Mom and Dad agreed she could stay at home to try and find Hercules!

Tuesday
So, no going back - we arrived at Grandad's this morning. There weren't any teary goodbyes from Mom when she dropped us off. We'd barely got our bags out the boot and she pretty much shouted bye out of the window and did a wheel spin as she sped away!

It had been a whole year since we last saw Grandad, and because it had been so long, as I knocked on the door, I started to feel a bit anxious about how I should say hello. David was fine, as he got away with a handshake. Whenever I greet people I always feel awkward, as I'm never too sure of the rules. I totally blame Dad for this. For as long as I can remember, instead of just having to say, 'hello' to friends and family, he gets me to hug them! 'Give them a hug,' are four words that make me break out into a cold sweat. I don't want to hug them! Hugging my parents can be painful at times, so I don't want to hug some random person who is apparently my cousin twice removed! I got so used to hugging people that came to the house, that I once tried to hug the guy who came round to fix our washing machine. I think he was pretty traumatised and left in a hurry.

So just as Grandad opened the door I made my decision, he was my Grandad and surely the rule was, I had to hug him. I went in for the hug, but then realised too late that Grandad was just trying to shake my hand. As I tried to pull out of the hug and go for the handshake instead, Granddad tried to give me a hug and we ended up head butting each other! It was so embarrassing, and I now have to wait a week before I can leave!

We walked into the lounge, and Grandad must have thought we were still 5 years old. Thomas the Tank Engine train set was all set up! David was too polite to upset Grandad, so thanked him and sat down. He looked ridiculous - a 16-year-old playing with Thomas & Friends!

I'm not sure how I contained my hysterics, but I shouldn't have been so quick to laugh, because next to my chair, I spotted a box of Sindy dolls and dresses! I was also too polite, and with nothing else to do anyway, I picked up Sindy and started trying on outfits. A couple of hours must have passed and David was doing an excellent job of convincing Grandad he was having a good time pushing Thomas around the track - maybe he actually was! I have to say, I secretly enjoyed dressing up Sindy in her numerous outfits - I won't ever be able to admit this to anyone - not even Ruby.

In the evening, I began to panic as Grandad told us the only TV channel he watches is 'Gold TV' - basically TV shows from at least a 100 years ago! We watched a couple of programs until Grandad announced it was now time to do the crossword and play Scrabble. I had never done a crossword and never heard of Scrabble - this was going to be a long week, was all I could think. Grandad absolutely thrashed us both at Scrabble, but when the best word I put down was 'cat' and David's was 'dog,' he didn't really have that much competition. Grandad is pretty clever though. He managed to complete the 'Super Tricky Crossword' by himself in only 10 minutes. I didn't realise old people could be so smart!

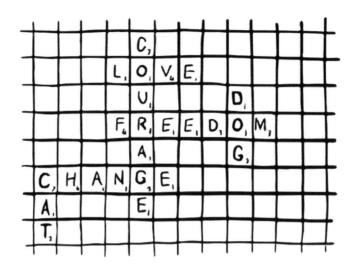

Wednesday

One good thing about this week, is that Grandad lets us get up at any time we want.

This morning it was 11am before I even peered over the top of my duvet! And when I went downstairs it was like Christmas had come early. On the kitchen table, were loads of variety cereal packs. At home we get two choices - weetabix or cornflakes - that's it! Now we had, cocoa pops, choco nut pillows, sugar puffs, honey nut loops – the lot!

Grandad seemed pretty pleased with himself when he saw my eyes nearly pop out of my head. I chose a mixture of cocoa pops and sugar puffs, but when I went to grab the milk, Grandad stopped me and handed me a jug of sweetened condensed milk. Well, all I can say, what a combination- heaven! I'm not too sure Mom and Dad would be impressed, but they weren't here to lecture me. But I could still hear Mom's voice in the back of my head, 'Too much sugar will put holes in your teeth and give you spots.' I'm certain this is just a myth anyway, like, 'You'll get square eyes if you watch too much TV.' And, 'You won't

35

be able to see in the dark if you don't eat your carrots.' I'm convinced parents just tell lies a lot of the time to get us to do stuff we don't want to do.

As well as all the cereal choices, there were packs of wagon wheels, jammy dogers, jars of chocolate spread, and a huge bowl of what he calls, 'The Lucky Dip.' This is basically every single bar of chocolate you can think of. He even had something called a 'Star bar'. After my cereal and 3rd 'Lucky Dip', I decided to call it a day as I was beginning to feel a bit unwell. After the initial sugar rush had worn off, I had to go and have a lie down - eating so much was exhausting!

When I eventually woke up, to my surprise, Grandad told us he had circuit training at 5pm, and could we go and watch. His doctor has apparently signed him up for 6 sessions after his last health check-up showed he needs to lose a few pounds. Without being unkind - Grandad does have a bit of a tummy on him. I think he may have caught me staring at it, because he keeps patting it and saying, 'full of wind.' But I'm beginning to think Grandad's, Lucky Dip, is not just for mine and David's benefit!

The big tummy was pretty much confirmed when we got into the car to go to his circuit class. He tried to put his seat belt on and asked me to help him pull more of the seatbelt out for him. But the seat belt had run out - there just wasn't enough to go round him! He made some comment about it being jammed and drove off. I was a bit worried that he wasn't safe, but then I thought his huge tummy would be the perfect air bag - just in case we did crash!

Luckily, we got there in one piece, although I'm not sure how. I was sat in the back and could see in the mirror that Grandad was driving with one eye shut! I'm not sure what that's all about, but probably not the best when you're driving a car!

When we arrived, I wasn't expecting any cross-fit champions, but some of the other participants made Grandad look like a gladiator. I've never seen so many zimmers in one place! There were 3 groups and Grandad was put in the bottom one because it was his first time. The circuit class was pretty basic - they just had to walk around four cones until the instructor said stop. Well, like I said, 'the zimmers' were no-where near as good as Grandad, but to be fair, one lady nearly overtook him on the last lap. So, before the end of the session, Grandad had been moved to the top group.

'I got promoted twice this evening,' he proudly said in the car on the way home. David and I said all the right things and told him he was brilliant, but he is a bit deluded. I know he is 80, but most of 'the zimmers' were in their 90's! I'm sure I read once that an 80-year-old climbed Mount Everest. Grandad has trouble climbing the stairs! When we got back to the house, he got over excited and announced he was going to do 20 press-ups!

Well, he went down for his first one and never made it back up! David and I had to try and haul him up, which involved pushing and pulling him in every direction. To make things worse though, Grandad would not stop farting! Every time we moved him into a different position he would let rip again! The stench was so bad, but there was no escape.

After about 10 minutes we eventually got him sitting in his chair and then made a run for it to try and detox our lungs. Maybe Grandad was right and his tummy was just full of wind!

Thursday
Me and David have weirdly been getting on okay. I suppose it's not so much as getting on, but we haven't been wanting to kill each other. There has been so much Lucky Dip and sleeping that there isn't enough time - or energy - to fight.

For breakfast today, we both ate a whole jar of Nutella - each!

Instead of getting cross, Grandad seemed really proud! But I think I over did it, because after the initial sugar rush, I started hallucinating – why was the lucky dip bowl sitting on Grandad's head?

After my afternoon nap, I was ready to start all over again with any other treats Grandad had for us, and he did not disappoint!

In the evening, he put on a barbecue for us. As well as the usual sausages and burgers, he introduced us to s'mores. Well, they are only the best thing I have ever tasted - a treat of toasted marshmallow and milk chocolate, sandwiched between two digestive biscuits. AMAZING!

The rest of the evening was really chilled, and I was beginning to think that being without my phone was not so bad after all. We did end up wasting a bit of time searching for Grandad's walking stick, until I realised I'd been using it to stoke the fire for the past two hours! To be fair it was dark, and it did look like just a regular stick. No harm done I thought, until I noticed Grandad looking a bit unbalanced as he walked into the house. I think I may have burnt a couple of inches off the bottom - oops!

Friday

DISASTER! I woke up this morning and thought I'd better brush my teeth after the Nutella and s'mores binge. I looked in the mirror and found a massive ZIT-ZILLA on my forehead! I tried to squeeze it, but it just made it bigger and bigger.

It was impossible to hide, so I went downstairs to get the teasing from David over and done with. He was going to have a field day I thought - 'Marjorie zit - zilla Egghead.' But my embarrassment turned to delight - he also had a zit-zilla - on the end of his nose! It was MASSIVE!!

It seems that Mom's warning about sugar giving you spots may be true after all. And I was beginning to get a throbbing pain in one of my back teeth. Maybe she's right about that too – too much sugar puts holes in your teeth!

Grandad was pretty shocked when he saw us but told us not to worry as he had a plan. He appeared with a milk bottle moments later and told us not to panic, as he could get rid of the zit with his milk bottle! So, his plan was, he would heat the milk bottle over a naked flame and place the opening of the bottle near the zit. The warm air from the bottle would act like a vacuum and suck out the zit into the bottle. My understanding of physics is zero and it seems five years studying it at school didn't make David any the wiser either, because he was unaware of this theory but was totally up for giving it a go. Luckily for me, David went first. So, milk bottle heated, Grandad held it carefully over the zit-zilla. I was waiting for an almighty splatter, as the zit got sucked into the bottle, but nothing happened. I could tell Grandad was getting a bit impatient, so he held the bottle a little closer. Then he suddenly shut one eye again - just like he did when he was driving! This time though, it must have caused a blind spot, because suddenly, the end of the bottle was on David's nose and stuck fast.

The scream that came out was like nothing I'd ever heard, and for a moment he seemed to hover off the chair with pain! Grandad - with now two eyes on the job - pulled heavily on the bottle and after several seconds it came off. But the zit hadn't gone, and now David had both the zit and a burn mark all around it. It was nasty! Thank goodness I didn't go first!

Saturday

This morning I stayed away from the 'Unlucky Dip,' and all the nasties alongside. I went for a bowl of yoghurt and fruit instead. It will take a whole lot of effort to get rid of this zit. David appeared later and also chose to stay away from the zit foods. He is going to need a miracle to get rid of his though. It's so red and angry, it looks like it could explode any second!

Grandad suggested salmon sandwiches for dinner, which sounded like a healthy option, even though I'd never tried one. But I sure won't be having one of those again. It was salmon out of tin with all the bones mashed in - super yuk!

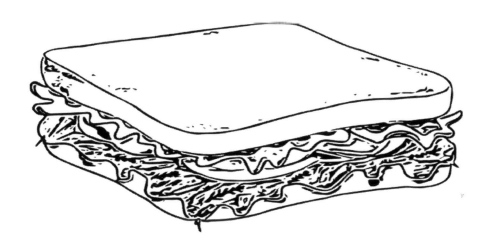

It's been an interesting week at Grandad's to say the least. And despite the zit and feeling I'm on the brink of getting diabetes, I did manage a whole week with no phone and not wanting to kill my brother. That is real progress! I'm even looking forward to seeing Emily! Even the digital detox was a success. But after my week at Grandad's, I now need a sugar detox.

Sunday

Mom picked us up from Grandad's and she did seem pleased to see us even with our killer zits. And her and Grandad are friends again – giving her a break for a whole week was definitely worth a pardon. I haven't seen Mom so happy in a long time. Are we really that bad?

Saturday

So back home and things are pretty good. Emily is out of my room! I think Mom was hoping I'd forgotten - not a chance! Her new 'room' is in the cupboard at the top of the stairs. I would describe it as a tight fit but cosy. They managed to squeeze most of her mattress in there, which was okay width wise, but about 30 cm short length wise. Her head sticks out into the hallway so this may be a bit inconvenient, but it's only until we move house and then we all get our own room.

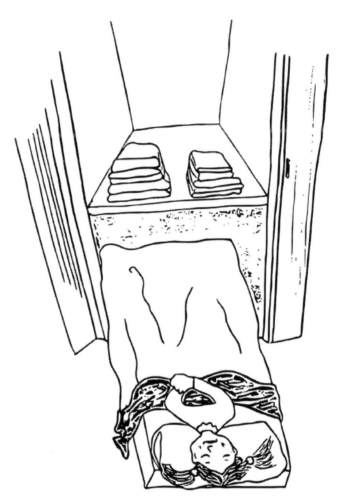

Monday

Having my own room at last is heaven! I do feel a bit guilty though. When I got up in the night to go to the toilet, I forgot Emily was there. I tripped up over her head on the way there and on the way back!

About half an hour later I heard Emily cry out, someone else got up and must have done the same – hopefully there is no lasting damage.

Wednesday

So, we thought Hercules had done a runner – never to be seen again, but it seems he may be hiding somewhere in the house. Mom found her super posh £50 mohair slippers annihilated this morning.

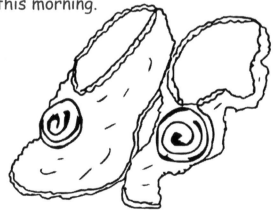

I reckon he must have used it to make his new bed - wherever that is?

Dad was also not happy. He couldn't cope with the thought of there being hamster poo all over the house. I think he is still having nightmares after he ate a load thinking it was raisins!

Friday
So today Mom bought another hamster for Emily to take to school next week, and Emily has to pretend it's Hercules. Mom is too embarrassed to tell the school that the real Hercules escaped, as apparently all the other Moms will be gossiping about it. So much for her telling us we must always be honest.

September

Sunday

Well, the 6 weeks holiday is over, and tomorrow is my first day at Chenet Secondary School. I suppose I'm kind of excited, but with a big dollop of fear added in too.

I guess it didn't help when I asked Mom earlier about her first day at secondary school. The 'Nube Annihilation Game,' is still her lasting memory of her first day and sounded awful! She was waiting on the playground with all the other year 7's for their tutors to collect them. While they waited, some older kids turned up from nowhere and surrounded them. They were rummaging through the bins, and before anyone had managed to work out what was happening, apple cores, banana peels, half eaten sandwiches and whatever else they could find, were launched at them!

Mom didn't get hit, but she saw one poor kid mis-time his duck and ended up with the remains of a mashed banana against the side of his head. Mom said he was spotted later in the day with a piece of it still perched inside his ear - gross!!!

I thanked Mom for her, NOT so re-assuring story and decided to make a quick exit when I could sense Dad was about to launch into one of his stories. I really didn't want to hear a repeat of, 'We used to climb trees when I was at school.' I'm pretty sure Dad's education involved more than climbing trees, but this is all he seems to remember. I mean it was so long ago, I'm not sure he can actually remember!

So, my top 3 fears for starting school are:

1.   **Nickname being found out**
2.   **Strict teachers**
3.   **Older kids**

I suppose as long as I stick to the rules, do my work and keep away from trouble, I'll be absolutely fine. What could possibly go wrong?

Monday

I survived my first day -just! I met Ruby at the top of the road and we walked to school together.

Apparently, her 'amazing' camper van holiday with her family was in fact a complete nightmare. All the photos she put on Instagram were just fake to make out she was having a good time. It seems this is what you have to do - fool everyone into thinking your life is perfect. I tried to make her feel better when I told her about my week at Grandad's house, but it didn't work. She said it sounded like an awesome week compared to what she went through. Right now though, we could see we had other problems - we noticed that most of the other girls walking to school had handbags - not rucksacks! We hadn't even arrived at school, and already I felt like I didn't fit in!

At school, we were collected from the hall by our tutor. Luckily, things have moved on since Mom was at school as there was no food flinging from the older kids. It seems though, that there is a new game - 'human ping pong.'

I came out of our tutor group at break time with the rest of the class to find loads of older kids - all boys - lined up like giants along each side of the corridor. Well, I knew for sure they weren't there to tell us, 'Welcome to your new school' just by the look on their faces. There was nowhere else to go - we had to go through them.

We got shoved from one side to the other, the whole length of the corridor! We then had the added pleasure of getting things pulled from our bags as we went along. I got my water bottle pulled out from mine - never to be seen again. I came off lightly though compared to Chinsen Chan; he had some spare pants pulled out of his bag!

How is he ever going to live that down? I saw him later asking where lost property was, trying to hunt them down – how embarrassing!

Thomas Lomas made the fatal mistake of saying he was going to tell. This Yeti lookalike just laughed at him with all his mates and said next time it will be 'speed ping pong' - just for him.
So, fear 2- fear of older kids - well and truly confirmed!

Being shoved to the back of the dinner queue is another 'treat' for us year 7's - basically we are the lowest of the low. Not only are we the youngest, but the smallest and weakest. I guess we just have to know our place - which is right at the bottom of the food chain - along with algae! Only another year until I can move up a level.

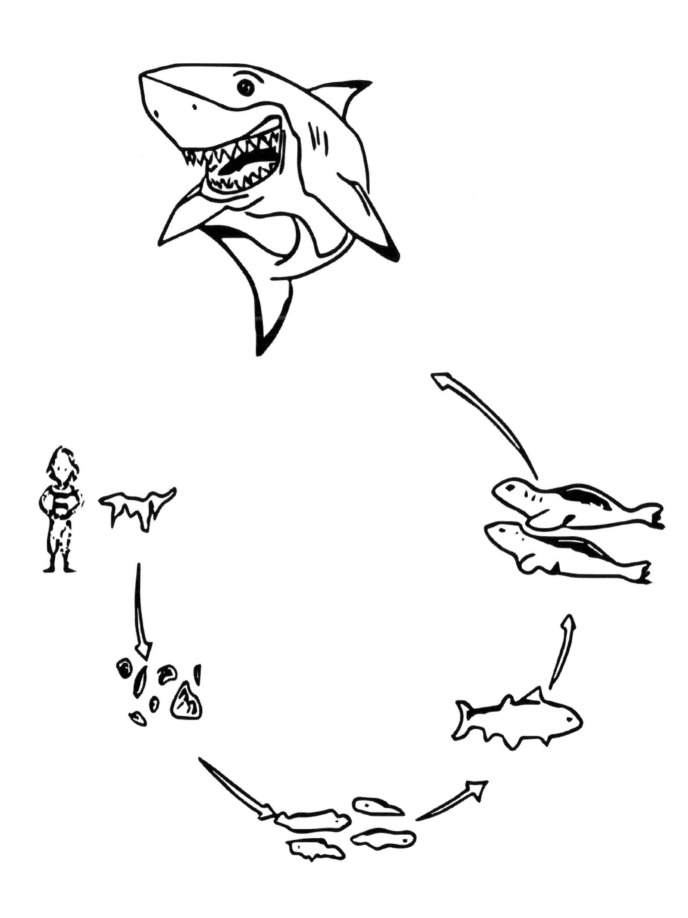

Tuesday

Seems like Mom is not up for getting me a handbag to replace the rucksack, even though I explained I would be the only one without. She said it's not practical and not necessary. Even when I told her I'd get picked on for having a rucksack as it's just not cool, she still wouldn't budge.

'I need to have a mind of my own,' she told me, 'And not follow the crowd' - does she not remember how school works?

Surprise, surprise, Ruby's Mom agreed to get her a handbag. Although Ruby is my best friend, she is really spoilt. The first time I went to her house - about 3 years ago - I could see how spoilt she was. She had her own mobile phone with unlimited data, £10 pocket money per week, a cupboard in the kitchen with treats - just for her and so many pairs of shoes I couldn't count. She was also pretty rude to her Mom, but she told me if you want nice things, you have to let parents know who's in charge. This did make sense at the time, and she convinced me to start putting my foot down with Mom and Dad.

So that night, I made a list of rules for Mom and Dad of how things would change. I asked for all the things that Ruby had: the phone, pocket money, new shoes and the treat cupboard

But my list of rules did not go down too well - they were ripped up and scattered over my head! Since then, I have to think carefully before I ask for anything.

Ruby - without doubt - will get her handbag and then I'll be the only non- nerd with a rucksack - great!!

Wednesday

Another day and I'm learning fast. A rubbish rule in secondary school is - can you believe? - we have to go outside for the whole of break and lunchtime! And get this, the teachers don't even let you stay behind in the classroom to do jobs. They are so ungrateful! When I offered to sharpen the pencils today for 3 of my teachers, I got, 'Out now!' I used to love sharpening the pencils and putting them in colour order! The problem is I hate the cold, so I'm going to have to come up with a plan. It's bearable now, but outside in November? - no thank you!!

Tuesday

I was so pleased today - me and Ruby got out of our lesson early and we were first in the lunch queue. But before we knew what was happening, a bunch of year 11's appeared and suddenly we were behind them! Not too bad, I thought, but then the year 10's, 9's and 8's appeared and then we were well and truly at the very back. It's probably just as well we have to wait until the end as I noticed some of the year 7's are buying food from the canteen as if they haven't eaten for a week. Mom and Dad learned the hard way with David when he first started at the school - he spent £50 in the canteen in the first week!

My maximum spend is £4 a day - and it must be, 'healthy' - basically boring stuff. Mom and Dad can even go on-line to check exactly what I'm eating. David managed to convince them for a whole year that a 'Traybake' was mixed vegetables baked in a tray until they phoned the school and found out that it was actually a selection of different cream cakes. I'm fine with healthy though as I'm probably still detoxing from my week at Grandad's. Some kids either have no restrictions or clueless parents as I noticed Sarah Lane in front of me, bought 10 cookies for £10!

Wednesday

Today, I used the school toilet for the first time. I won't be doing that again!
I'm going to have to train myself to only go before and after school.

I wasn't expecting triple-ply quilted loo roll, but I thought basic hygiene wasn't
too much to ask for. After getting lost - fear number 3 confirmed - I
eventually found the COMMUNAL toilets!

I should have known there and then it would be a war zone.

The first toilet had 3 whole toilet rolls shoved down it, the second had no seat,
the third toilet had no lock, so loo 4 was my only option.
I was okay until I tried to walk out of the cubicle. My feet wouldn't move
because my shoes were stuck to the floor - from dried pee! And this could only
be boy's pee - gross!

And just to finish this traumatic experience off, as I stood washing my hands, a huge clump of wet loo paper which had been thrown onto the ceiling, became dislodged and hit me smack on my head. So not only did I have a faint whiff of stale pee coming from me - thanks to the sticky shoes - but I had bits of wet toilet paper stuck in my hair.

Last lesson was PE, so at least I could change out of my pee encrusted shoes. I like PE and I've never understood why it's not more popular with everyone else. You don't have to read, write, or work out any tricky sums - easy! If you don't like it though, there are no excuses allowed- not like in primary school. Amy Matthews tried to get out of today's cross-country lesson by saying, she'd forgotten her kit. Last year, all you needed to say was, 'I've hurt my little finger' and you'd get to sit it out - it was so easy to get away with. But not now it seems. Amy had to find some kit from lost property, and it looked like it had been festering there for years - stinking, dirty and mouldy - someone else's kit! Gross!! I bet she won't ever forget her kit again!

Thursday

Since Monday, I've been noticing that some of my teacher's faces change - for the worse - whenever they get to my name in the register. At first, I thought I was just imagining it.

But by third lesson, it was now obvious - a mix of pain and dread would spread over their face, and it was just when my name was called. I thought they may have spotted my middle name, but surely teachers can't be that mean?

Eventually, I was put out of my misery, or should I say, my misery was just beginning! Mr Barratt, the Science teacher explained it with 1 simple question. I should have lied but I felt my cheeks go bright red as I admitted to the family connection. Trying to shake off his reputation when he'd had 5 years to leave his mark was going to be tough! By last lesson, I had sweated so much with the stress of being asked, I think I may have had body odour! Luckily, I was sitting next to Paul Wild - Wild by name and wild by nature - who always has a permanent stench around him, so I just kept pointing my head in his direction when people started complaining.

Friday
So, after my first week at school, I think I'm beginning to understand what behaviour is okay and what is not. It's like an unwritten rule book that has always been there.

It is amazing how things change as you go through school. In reception, no one really cares what you look like, sound like or even smell like! By year 3 there is a bit of a change, but by year 7 - Bam! There are very clear rules, and if you fail to understand them - you're doomed!

Reception Rules	Year 3 Rules	Year 7 Rules
Holding hands with mom/dad on the way to school - OK	No hand holding, but mom/dad can walk beside you.	No mom/dad allowed within a 50- metre radius
Hair that is long, short, curly, straight greasy, dry or full of nits - OK	Everything still fine apart from the nits.	Only the latest trendiest hairstyle
Having a snotty nose and eating it - OK	Snot allowed, but no eating it!	Snot or boggys even if still inside nose - not allowed
Extra body tissue eg warts extra toes/fingers - OK	Warts are fine but must be covered.	Any kind of extra body tissue eg, warts - absolutely not allowed
Themed, fluffy pencil cases of any colour for boys and girls - OK	No pink for boys, but fine for girls	No pencil case at all seems the best option. The coolest option is the inside of your blazer pocket.
Begging the teacher to give you a job - OK	Doing jobs for the teacher without complaining.	Doing anything that is deemed helpful to any teacher or member of staff - Not allowed
Sending the teacher Christmas presents/end of year presents and saying you love them - OK	Presents are ok, but no mention of love.	No gratitude in any form to any teacher allowed.

The one I'm gutted about the most is the stationery. In year 6, Mom and Dad bought me the most amazing pencil case, with pencils that smell of bubble gum and apples, and rubbers that smell of and look like chocolate and strawberry milkshakes. All week I've been trying to show off my latest blueberry smelling pencil, but I noticed the coolest kid in the class - Isobel Price - just had the inside bit of a biro with the plastic case gone. My pink, sequinned sparkling pencil case that has a built-in pencil sharpener and calculator, suddenly did not seem so cool. I sensed a few looks on the first day, which I thought were looks of admiration. By today though, I sussed out that every time my pencil case appeared, the sniggers would start. Luckily, a few other kids had made the same mistake, and had even gone a step further. Amelia Howlett had a seaside themed pencil case with similar pens and pencils as me - although her pencils had her name on. Her one step further was that she also had a lunch box and water bottle to match! This used to be the coolest thing to have at primary school - how things can suddenly change.

When I got home, I gave the whole lot to Emily. Well, I didn't just give it to her. She happily agreed to be my foot-rest for 30 minutes while I watched TV.

Monday

It turns out that being 'ping- ponged' down the corridor is not a one-off 1st day or week welcome for the year 7's.

It's now week 2 and the giants don't seem to be letting up. Today it took me twice as long to get to each lesson. I was pushed from left to right down the corridor and ended up late for my next lesson. Don't these kids have lessons to go to? Why are they always there no matter what? Luckily, my new un-themed water bottle was secure in my bag, which has a lock on, so nothing was taken. Chinsen Chan seems to be one of those people who don't learn from their mistakes. Another pair of pants were pulled out of his bag today - with Batman on them! The year 11's took great delight in throwing them round the corridor singing 'Duna , duna, duna, duna Batman!' This poor kid - someone needs to tell him!

Hey loser, where's Robin?

It then soon came to a sudden end when one of the giants who had the pants on his head smelt something dodgy. He quickly took them off his head to reveal a brown stain on his forehead. He won't be trying that again in a hurry!

I had music last lesson and found out that Mom has put me down to have trombone lessons after school without even asking me!
Of all the instruments, she picked the trombone - I'm furious! The lessons are voluntary, even though I 100% did not volunteer. Mom signed me up for 12 taster sessions, paid for up front, so I have to take them. Apparently, she tried to get me guitar lessons, but they were already full. At least the guitar would have been more practical and sociable - I'm never going to pull a trombone out around the campfire and kick out a few tunes! Not cool!

Tuesday

Got my first detention today - along with Ruby - for nearly drowning! How is that fair! We were doing synchronised swimming in our PE Lesson - basically dancing - or in our case - drowning in the water!

We weren't the only ones who got a detention though. Shirley Parks - another one who didn't learn from our last PE lesson, tried to get out of it by saying she'd left her swimming stuff at home. Poor Shirley. It appears that the lost property box extends to swim wear too! She went pale as she rooted through a bunch of crusty, stinking, thread bear costumes. I dread to think who has worn them and how many wees must have been done in them!

She tried to explain there were none her size, but five minutes later, Shirley appeared in a costume that was so small and see through it was almost obscene! As well as the embarrassment, she got a detention for, 'Lack of equipment.'

The lesson itself was actually good fun at first - better than cross-country anyway! We had to make up a routine in pairs that had 5 different synchronised swimming techniques. I was with Ruby, and all was going well until we attempted the backward somersault to compete our routine. We moved into position but made the mistake of looking at each other for a nano second just before we went backwards. We both laughed and then went backwards in the water with no air in our lungs.

Let's just say being underwater with no spare air is not a good idea! We came up coughing and spluttering - and laughing. We just about managed to swim to the side before we choked to death! The detention was for, 'Disturbing the learning of others' - how unfair is that! 'I'm very sorry if I nearly drowned and it affected others from learning,' is what I wanted to say to Miss, but thought I'd better leave it- knowing my luck I'd end up with a double detention!

Halloween

It was only a few of years ago that Halloween seemed to be a, take it or leave it celebration, but now it's massive! Loads of free sweets and chocolate for just a couple of hours of knocking on doors in a scary costume, is a piece of cake and the best night ever!
Last year though, Ruby and me had a few problems in getting some of the locals to hand over the sweets. Because there were so many kids out trick and treating, they were only giving the sweets to the younger kids. Half the houses last year told me and Ruby we were too old, so this year, we got Emily to tag along. Can you believe though - I had to make a deal with her: if I got any sweets, I would have to give her half!

The other problem we had last year was that some scallywags were stealing all the sweets left on people's doorstep, so by the time we arrived there were no sweets left. This year though I came prepared - I had a card machine! It was only £25 to buy and as long as I broke even I would have it for next year too and be quids in!

It seemed like a great idea, because if the sweets ran out, I could suggest, 'that's no problem as I also take cash or card - whatever is easier.' But when I presented the card machine where the sweets had run out, it seemed to make most people pretty cross. And when I explained it was a £1 minimum donation, they didn't seem too keen at all.

Get out of here, or I'll call the police!!

So, with zero donations, I was £25 down and after giving half the sweets to Emily, I was left with a lame collection of treats.

November

Wednesday
Maths is suddenly getting really tricky and very boring. Today was probably the most boring maths lesson ever! Seriously, in the real world, when will I ever need to know the area of a circle? So, I was staring out of the classroom window, praying the lesson would end, when I spotted a super cool year 11 girl. She had a leather jacket, rolled up skirt, red lipstick and several piercings.

I nudged Ruby to take a look, and the two of us looked on at the coolest girl ever! She strutted across the playground like she owned it - I wished I could be like that. Tomorrow me and Ruby have agreed we are going to roll up our skirts up and see if we can find some of our Mom's red lipstick - we can look cool too!

Thursday

Well, Ruby and me managed to get another detention, AND our eyes nearly poked out today. The red lipstick and the rolled-up skirt are apparently against the school policy. We didn't even make it past the school gate. The Head was there with a ruler in hand. Any skirt that looked even slightly short was measured. We were 10.6 cm too short and had a lot of unrolling to do.

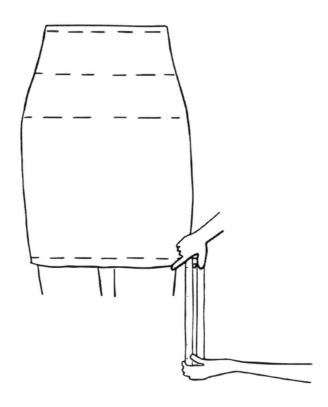

By 8:50 am - Lippy was washed off and skirt back to correct length. It's so unfair, how does the cool girl get away with it!
We didn't realise at the time, but the detention was the least of our worries. What we hadn't realised yesterday, while we were staring at super cool girl, was that she spotted both of us staring right at her.

Maths had just ended when I spotted cool girl outside, and she seemed to be glaring back at us with a pretty mad look on her face. Ruby and me went to make a dash for the door, but everyone in front of us was moving so slowly. Then she was in the doorway, and we knew we were in big trouble! We began moving back, but - too late - we were cornered. Everyone else had left the room; she had us. Now, I can't write down what she actually said, so I will use the word 'fruity' for the bad words.

'If either of you fruity girls ever so much as glance at me again, (her 2 fingers from each hand were now raised and only a cm from our eyes), I will poke your fruity eyes out.'

A very clear message and another rule - no eye contact with the cool girl.

Friday

It seems the giants do not appear to be getting bored of 'human ping pong.' At first, it seemed the best option was to make a run for it. But then Darrell Doiley got tripped halfway along, and did a massive face plant, so that idea is now out. The cameras that overlook the corridors must be dummies, otherwise, surely the teachers would stop it- unless they're all in the staff room huddled round the cameras getting entertained at our expense.

One of the year 7's though, has adapted quite well to the 'ping-pong.' He is quite small, so that helps. As he approaches the giants, he goes down on his hands and knees and scurries through everyone's legs on all 4's. Every time he manages to make it through unscathed.

Monday

Do you remember when I said me and Ruby don't like going outside for break and lunch? Well, I've come up with a genius plan. Outside the library today, there was a notice asking for librarians to help out during break and lunch time. We've already filled in the application form and will find out next week. We both had to lie a bit though, so I hope we don't get found out. One question was, 'What was the last book you read?' I didn't think it would look too good if I put down, 'We're Going On a Bear Hunt.' I really don't like telling lies, but equally I don't like looking dumb, so instead I put down, 'To Kill a Mockingbird' Mom has been pestering me to read it for ages. Apparently, it's a classic - whatever that means? Ruby had the same problem as me. The last book she read was, 'The Gruffolo,' so she put down, 'Romeo and Juliet' - I told her that was an obvious lie, and she should tone it down, but she wouldn't listen! We will find out next week if we're in.

Friday

Today we had our first lesson of Lifeskills - basically common-sense stuff. I thought it would be dead easy, but it seems there is still lots to learn. Unfortunately, I ended up making a complete fool of myself. But I am trying to pull it off as just trying to be funny.

The topic was tax, and the question, 'What does VAT stand for on our shopping receipts?' I remembered watching this 80's program on Gold TV when I was at Grandad's, called 'Minder.' The main character walked into the pub and asked the man behind the bar for a VAT so I asked Grandad what this meant. He explained VAT is short for vodka and tonic - an alcoholic drink.
Grandad is so clever; I was sure it must be right. I put my hand up and proudly answered, 'Vodka and Tonic.' But vodka and tonic was not the same VAT as Mr Newman was talking about, and his glare told me he was not impressed. Of course, Mark Gilbury-Smith - Smug Smithy - got the correct answer, 'Value Added Tax Sir.' It was then obvious my answer was wrong - why would an alcoholic drink be printed on people's receipts?

I felt myself go red with embarrassment. It really didn't help when Smug Smithy told me I was going red. I really didn't need him to tell me - I was well aware my cheeks were on fire!

And to top off my humiliation, I got another lunchtime detention for, 'Disruption during classroom activities.'

Saturday

So next week is my birthday - 12 years old! and I've been looking forward to it for ages, even though it will be a quiet one. I wanted a pool party, but Mom and Dad were having none of it. 'No more parties,' apparently now I'm in secondary school! I love parties, as it means loads of presents. Thinking about it though, Mom and Dad have never been that keen - I remember finding Mom crying after my 9th birthday party. She convinced me at the time it was because she was sad the party had finished, but I think it was because she hated every minute of it.

And Dad would often go missing at most of my parties - his excuse I remember - he was preparing the party games, but I'm pretty sure he used to lock himself in the loo!

Now I'm at secondary school, I've been told, it's 3 friends for a takeaway and a film - pretty dull, but better than nothing I suppose. Looks like I have to say farewell to the days when we hired out halls, swimming pools and bowling alleys.

Saturday
Well so much for a great birthday - Mom and Dad - more Dad - pretty much ruined it! Ruby, Rachel and Amy came round at 6pm and Mom and Dad promised to make themselves scarce, so we could all chill out in the lounge for the evening. But after only an hour, Dad couldn't help himself, so nipped downstairs to check on us. When he saw us all on our phones, he gave us a lecture on how we needed to be be more sociable and not be so addicted to our phones. He left, but an hour later he came down again and when he saw us still on them, and can you believe - he confiscated all our phones! He said when we had finished the film and discussed the best bits, we could have our phones back! I was so embarrassed! I didn't go red, but I felt myself go icy white and on the verge of passing out! My friends are going to think I'm the biggest loser ever!

Sunday

I'm still so cross from yesterday, so today I decided to get my own back on Dad. Parents are so dumb when it comes to technology, so it was pretty obvious what to do - I downloaded the TV remote control onto my phone. Dad was watching his football team play in some kind of qualifying game. It was 1-1 after extra time and had now gone onto penalties. I crouched down next to the crack in the lounge door and waited patiently. After the first few penalties were taken, I was delighted to hear just how excited Dad was. With the last penalty about to be taken, the whole game depended on this strike. Now! Suddenly, the penalty shoot-out disappeared and Tinky Winky from the Tellytubbies appeared, riding her scooter up and down the green hills. I nearly choked from trying not to laugh. Dad was frantically pressing the remote control, having the biggest melt down ever!

It has been quite amusing listening to Dad complaining to Mom about how there is something wrong with his new TV. It was even more amusing listening to him on the phone at 8 am this morning, complaining to the poor sales assistant that his new TV was broken.

Monday

Getting from lesson to lesson, sure is tricky business - not just because of the 'human ping pong,' but the amount we have to cart around. We were spoilt at primary school - we had all our lessons in the same classroom. We had trays to put all our books in, a coat peg to hang coats and PE kit on, trays for water bottles, and now - nothing! Today I had PE, cookery and my trombone lesson. So, I was like a cart horse trying to carry all my stuff. Every time I turned a corner, I kept taking people out!

Well, one bit of good news today was that me and Ruby are the new year 7 librarians. I did get caught out though when Miss Dewer looked at my application form and asked me my favourite part in, 'To Kill a Mockingbird.' I immediately felt my face go red as I desperately thought of a likley answer. At the time, I thought I sounded quite convincing, 'I'm not too sure of my favourite bit Miss, but I would say my least favourite bit is when the Mockingbird dies.' I could tell from the expression on her face it was definitely the wrong answer.

She then asked Ruby the same question. Ruby looked really confident as she explained her favourite part in Romeo and Juliet, 'Well it has to be when they get married and live happily ever after.' My face was now beetroot. Surely everyone knows the basic Romeo and Juliet story? Miss Dewer looked seriously unimpressed, but must have been desperate as she said we could start on Monday.
I got home later and did a bit of research. Apparently, there is no mocking bird in, 'To Kill A Mockingbird,' or any other birds for that matter. It is symbolic! I was too tired to look up what that meant.

Monday
So, we have been librarians for a week, and I think we knew it was never going to be the most exciting job, but anything is better than being outside in the cold. Today, Ruby was even more bored than me. She made up a game to find the biggest nerd in the library and give them a shock by creeping up behind them and whacking them on the head with a book - 'knock the nerd' she called it.

Noughts and crosses or hangman would have passed the time I'm sure, but she insisted it would be fun. The idea of course was not to get caught. To be fair, it did manage to entertain us both for the whole of break and lunch and there were plenty of nerds to choose from. Ruby's theory is that the great thing about nerds is that they may be clever, but they can't usually run, so she's never going to get caught!

Tuesday

Another one of Ruby's theories is that the lower down the school you are, the more effort you make to get to lesson. The year 8's and 9's, sometimes walk quickly. Years 10 and 11 seem to be in no rush at all. For them it's almost like - the last one to arrive at lesson is the coolest!

This is very different for us year 7's. I do try and walk as quickly as I can, but for some it's like a full sprint as soon as you leave one lesson to get to the next. And if you need the toilet in between - you've had it! I saw Spencer Taylor today run out of the toilets still pulling his trousers up, half-way down the corridor!

Wednesday

I was so close to getting another detention today from the most feared teacher in the school -Tomkinson! I was outside class waiting for our teacher to arrive when I noticed two older kids at the top of the stairs looking down and giggling. And so it turned out to be a definite case of curiosity killed the cat! I walked over, and these kids ran off. I looked down the stairs to see a load of torn up paper floating down - right onto Mr Tomkinson's head! He looked up - directly at me - and I knew I was in for it. He may be the shortest teacher in the school, but he is without doubt, the most feared. The warning, 'Leg it, it's Tomkinson,' came too late, but I ran into the classroom and sat right at the back hoping he wouldn't see me.

He slowly entered the room, and everyone sat in silence as he scanned the room. He found me within seconds, and I could hear my heart beat pounding in my head. His eyes locked onto me, and I swear they went red for a second. He walked towards me, and I think I'd stopped breathing at this point. In the quietest of voices with every word emphasised, he hissed, 'One day Pickering, I'm going to tell you what I think of you.' Now, this sounds like I got off lightly, but I was so scared, I very slightly peed myself! Luckily - no detention this time.

Thursday

So, it appears Ruby may have taken her 'Knock the Nerd' game a bit too far today and it may have been partly my fault, because without realising I handed Ruby an encyclopaedia instead of your average size book.

She followed her nerd into a corner and seemed to struggle as she lifted the book - it was so heavy. As soon as she lifted it, I saw her panic slightly as she lost control and gravity took over. With one huge smack, she managed to knock the nerd out stone cold! We panicked – we thought he was dead! Luckily, he started moving and was murmouring, 'Where am I.' Ruby told me to get him some water, but I didn't realise it was for him to drink it and I threw it over his face - oops!

Word quickly got out about what happened, and by the end of the day, several complaints were received by Miss Dewer saying that they were being ambushed in the library from behind, and this may have been the case for the latest victim. So, Miss Dewer decided the library would be closed until further notice. To be honest, I'm not that bothered; I think I prefer being out in the cold than sitting in that library with all those books. They really were beginning to give me a headache.

Friday

After yesterday's drama, I thought it best to really knuckle down and focus on my work. I was doing pretty well until we had English last lesson. English on a Friday afternoon though is never a good idea as most of us can barely string a sentence together.

The lesson objective today - 'Write a Sea Disaster story.' I had my story in my head almost straight away, so I switched off when Miss Beamont asked the class for ideas. I was still switched off when I suddenly heard Miss Beaumont say my name, 'Helen, they have a good sense of what?' I had absolutely no idea what she was talking about. I looked around in panic, hoping someone would mouth the answer to me, but nothing. Ruby obviously hadn't been listening either as I got a completely blank face from her. So, I answered the first thing that came into my head, 'Humour, Miss.' As I was saying it, I realised that a 'Disaster at Sea' story probably wouldn't involve any humour, but it was too late. Everyone burst out laughing - apart from Mrs Beaumont. I found out after the lesson that the crucial bit of the question that I missed was, 'Sharks have a good sense of what?' I still cannot believe I said humour!

This was a disaster lesson in more ways than one for me - a detention for 'Lack of effort'. So, to make up for it I wrote a gripping story that is sure to impress. I really can't afford to get any more detentions, because I won't be able to go on the end of term trip to Alton Towers - only the best theme park ever.

Monday

Some of my teachers I've decided are a bit odd. First there's my RE teacher - Mrs Baker. She sets us work to copy from the board - for the whole lesson - and spends the rest of the lesson knitting. I'm all for relaxing and taking it easy, but I'm pretty sure this is not allowed.

Some of the other kids are massively taking advantage of this. It started off with just talking, passing notes and doing very little work. Then a few weeks later, people were on their phones and listening to music with ear pods in. But this week they have taken it to another level. Tyler Taylor brought a waffle machine in from home and was making and selling waffles at the back of the class!

Then there's the ICT teacher - Mr Russell. He drinks at least 4 cans of cola during the lesson and seems to be on a permanent sugar rush. Today, I googled it and that's 27 teaspoons of sugar - just in 1 lesson!

Mr Broadbent, the science teacher is really strange. He sometimes lies down during the lesson on the bench at the front of the classroom and tells us we are all boring. He says we have to be more enthusiastic about his lessons, otherwise he will just lie down and be boring like the rest of us! I'm actually fine with this - I hate science.

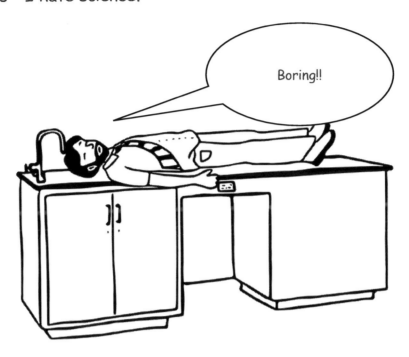

Mrs Gill, the art teacher is pretty rude really. And she laughs at her own jokes which are really bad. In our lesson today, Timmy Parks - who is the smallest boy in the entire school, went to her desk and asked if he could have a tissue. Mrs Gill told him he couldn't have one because they were, 'man-size,' tissues. She then laughed for about 2 minutes, delighted at her terrible joke.

Next, there is Mr Alban-Jones, who is Head of PE. We have him for fitness every week and most people dread it more than any other lesson. He calls us all by our surnames - which is fine by me, as long as it's not the middle name!

There are never any sick notes though or, 'I forgot my kit Sir.' If you are even a second late for his lesson, he makes you do a 5km run as a punishment!

Apparently, he used to be an officer in the Royal Navy, and every opportunity he gets, he likes to remind us. When we had our first gym lesson, he roared at us to get 'starboard side.' Well, everyone just looked at each other completely clueless. Then he called us a bunch of morons - which I'm quite certain he's not allowed to do. Starboard was the right side of the gym he told us, and the last person there would do 20 press ups. Well, you can imagine how quickly we all moved. Poor Shirley was always going to be last. She managed 2 press ups before collapsing in a heap. I would say he needs to work on his motivation skills.

Then today, it was poor Amy Dickens I felt sorry for - she was 5 minutes late for the lesson. She explained to Sir, that on her way to school, an old lady had taken a fall, so she stopped to help until the ambulance arrived. Sir told her he was feeling kind and would let her off the 5km run, but only if she found the old lady and got her to do it instead! The guy is a nutcase!

Tuesday

We got our English marks back today and it seems Mrs Beamont was not very impressed with my Sea Disaster story. It was actually based on a true story, so I was convinced it would be very believable. It happened to Dad when he was around my age. He was at the beach with his family and decided to take a dip in the sea. Ten metres in, he suddenly spotted a giant poo heading straight for him. He tried to get away from it, but it seemed to be chasing him - as if it had a mind of its own.

I'm going to get you!

In his panic to get away, he lost his footing from underneath him and went under the water. Dad stood up, just as the giant poo floated over the top of his head. It now sat…. on the top of his head! The beach cleared as poor Dad ran crying back to his Mom and Dad.

I honestly cannot think of a sea disaster worse than this, but I got a lunchtime detention for 'Lacking the required standards.' Mrs Beamont made me read the story out to the class and warned anyone who laughed, would be joining me for detention. And if I dared to laugh, it would be a double detention! Well, telling someone they're not allowed to laugh is the worst thing you can do. My cheeks burned red as I stood at the front of the class and read my story aloud. I looked up at one point and saw all the nerds tutting and shaking their heads in disgust. Smug Smithy looked the most disgusted of all. But then I made the mistake at looking at Ruby who had silent tears pouring down her face and was biting her hand to try and stop herself from laughing. Well, when I saw her, I could no longer contain myself. My voice stumbled, then the tears and finally a huge roar of laughter. It was a detention for Ruby and a double detention for me!

Wednesday
That nerd Smug Smithy has been annoying me for weeks with his sarcastic comments about sharks having a great sense of humour and how I'm always going red. So, today, it would have been difficult for anyone not to have done the same in my position. On the way back from the toilet, I saw him walking towards me in the corridor - carrying a load of textbooks piled high.

I walked past him, but then couldn't resist. I turned around and gave him a quick but firm nudge - from behind. At first, he managed to hold onto the books by stumbling forward, trying to get his balance. But a few seconds later, the whole lot went down - with him underneath - it was brilliant! I was out of view by the time he turned around, so I think I've got away with it! I can't afford anymore detentions.

Thursday

Well, so much for the cameras in the corridors being dummies - apparently not! My quick nudge yesterday was caught on a very much working camera. A grovelling letter to Smithy and another detention was my punishment. It was totally worth it though! How come the 'human ping-pong' isn't getting spotted then? There must be hours of 'ping -pong' on camera. I do a nano second nudge and get busted!

Monday

Can things get much worse for me? Apparently so! After assembly today, all those who were doing the winter camp trip, were asked to stay behind. Losers, I thought, who on earth would voluntarily go on a camp that involves walking in the freezing cold? But I couldn't believe it when I heard, 'Pickering, where are you going?' from Mr Alban-Jones. I tried to explain there was some mistake as I didn't want to go. But Sir told me that Mom had emailed him directly asking to sign me up. He handed me a permission slip to take home for Mom and Dad to sign for the 3-day trip! First trombone lessons and now this. Why does my mother keep volunteering me for things I absolutely do not want to do!

At home, after lots of ranting at Mom and Dad, I knew it was useless. After so many detentions, they thought this would be a good way to sort me out and would be a good life experience. Walking for 3 days in the middle of winter is my idea of torture!

Tuesday

I can't go on my own with a bunch of walking nerds, so somehow, I'll have to convince Ruby to sign up. The permission slip has to be in tomorrow, so I have 24 hours to convince her. My persuasive list:

1. Three days of fresh air
2. Exercise is enjoyable
3. Beautiful scenery
4. Great fun with me
5. A few days off school
6. No chores to do at home - even though she doesn't do any anyway
7. Staying in a posh hotel

A great list I thought, but I couldn't help but think of what it would be really like:

1. Two days of dull walking
2. Trying to work out how to read a map
3. Cold and miserable surroundings
4. Spending 3 days with walking nerds - only nerds are going
5. Sleeping in a dormitory on a grotty bed

Wednesday

So, I gave her the list, but the look on her face told me she was not convinced. There is no way I'm going with all those nerds on my own, so I need a backup plan. It was pretty simple really. I will leave the permission slip at home, knowing tomorrow is the last day to hand it into Sir.

Thursday

Well, today is going down as the most embarrassing day of my whole life!!
There is no way out of this, I'm going to have to leave school!
I was sitting in a whole school assembly at the very front. The headteacher
was wittering on about something when I heard a commotion at the back of the
hall. At first, I didn't turn around, but as the noise carried on, I glanced
behind - along with the rest of the school. GASP, SHOCK, HORROR! it was my
flipping mother! I suddenly felt violently sick, and I literally wanted to die
there and then. Mr Hind stopped reading and the whole of assembly went
silent. Then eyes were on me. I slowly stood and walked towards her - cheeks
burning so badly, I could feel that heartbeat in my head again! Then I heard
my mother, I attempted a weak smile, my plan had backfired big time! Now I
was going on winter camp as well as looking a total fool!

Darling, your permission slip for the winter camp... I found it!!

Friday
The only good thing about yesterday, is that Ruby felt so sorry for me after what Mom did, she decided she would come on the winter camp trip. She really is the bestest friend.

Saturday
Today I found out that for David's 17th birthday, which is tomorrow, he is getting a proper party - Paintballing! Everyone kept that one quiet!
Mom and Dad explained that they agreed to it, as it was to prepare him for the Army, otherwise it would have been the same as what I got - please don't remind me! Emily gets to watch as she's too young, but the rest of us are having to take part to make up the numbers. Aunty Trudy - Dads' sister and Uncle Alex - the highly competitive brother-in-law are coming too. It may actually turn out to be very entertaining, as Dad and Uncle Alex are always trying to outdo each other - in everything. Sometimes in sport, or just petty things like, who has the smartest sunglasses or best iPhone.

To be honest though, Dad has pretty much given up on most of the sports competitions, as last year he really hurt his back. It was partly Mom's fault - she had managed to persuade Dad to join the gym. The idea came after watching her favourite movie, 'Dirty Dancing.' Mom decided she would like her own Patrick Swayze - the main character - who has big muscles as well as being a brilliant dancer. But Mom's idea massively backfired as Dad apparently went too heavy and tried to squat the equivalent of a baby rhino on his back.

Instead of looking like Patrick Swayze, he looked more like Grandad. He had a walking stick for about 3 weeks and couldn't go anywhere without it. Every now and again, his back will seize up again and he goes back to doing a great impression of Grandad!

Recently, Dad went for the 'petty things' route to try and get one over on Uncle Alex. He bought a new TV - the one that got sucker smacked by the toy bow and arrow - hoping it would be bigger and better than Uncle Alex's. Unfortunately, Dad made the mistake of showing off the new TV on the family WhatsApp group, as soon as he got it out the box. This just gave Uncle Alex time to think of how to go bigger and better.

A few weeks later when we went to their house, Dad was feeling all smug and couldn't wait to tell Uncle Alex about his new 55-inch TV. We couldn't even see their TV when we first walked into the lounge and Dad must have thought Uncle Alex had accepted defeat. But then Dad spotted the projector hanging from the ceiling - then looked opposite and saw the rolled-up screen. I honestly saw the blood run out of his face. With one quick flick, Uncle Alex announced, 'Check this out!' The projector screen slowly came down - 120 inches! - more than twice as big as Dad's. Well and truly beaten!

94

Later that day, things just got worse for poor Dad. They were playing golf at Uncle Alex's posh golf club. Dad had practised his swing at the local driving range in the week, and luckily his back was holding out. But Uncle Alex had erected some new golf nets in his back garden and was able to practise all day long. And just to finish things off, Uncle Alex had bought himself a remote-controlled golf bag so didn't have to carry his clubs around the course. By the time they'd done 18 holes, Dad was doing his Grandad impression again!

Sunday

So today was David's paint balling party and by the end of the day, I had become a bit of a hero with Dad and David! But not so popular with Uncle Alex. I'll explain. Team 1 was: me, Uncle Alex, Charlie our cousin and Mom, along with 4 other random guys. Team 2 was: David, Dad, Aunty Trudy and Joe our cousin, along with another 4 random guys. Anyway, my team - mainly thanks to Uncle Alex - were absolutely annihilating Team 2 in the first game, very much to the annoyance of Dad. By the end of the game, I'd had enough - let me tell you, getting hit by a paint ball, really, really hurts! So instead of being where all the action was, for the next games, I decided to find somewhere quiet and as far away as possible to sit it out. In my secluded ditch, instinct took over when I saw someone near me in the bushes sniping away - so I shot them! Each time it was Uncle Alex! I'd managed to take him out of the game 3 times by the time he spotted me in my ditch. He was pretty mad.

So, by eliminating the sniper so many times, Team 1 won. I really didn't mind that I was on the losing team. It felt good to have played a part in Dad getting one over Uncle Alex - it has been a long time coming! I have to say, Dad was not so gracious in his victory.

December

Saturday

Now David is 17 he has started to learn to drive and has had a few lessons with his driving instructor. So far, he has managed not to crash the car. I just can't imagine him being that good - he's so lanky and uncoordinated. This morning, Mom thought it would be a good idea if Dad took him to practise. 'It will be a good chance for the two of you to bond,' said Mom. Well, her idea has not really worked. I watched out of my bedroom window to see how long Dad would last before telling him to get out. My prediction of 'to the end of the road' was even way off. At first David seemed to be doing well and reversed slowly down the driveway, almost perfectly, but then disaster! He must have panicked, because he remained in reverse, with his foot full on the accelerator! He shot down the rest of the driveway like a bullet and went the all the way to the top of next door's driveway. How he didn't knock over and demolish their wall, I'll never know. Dad was white when he got out the car and the vein had well and truly popped up!

Monday

So, it's finally here, winter camp! We arrived at school at 8:30 am and as we were loading our stuff onto the minibus, I realised I'd forgotten my sleeping bag! It was too late for Mom to go back and get it, so Sir came to the rescue with his DOG'S blanket out the back of his car! Gross! It was covered in hair and slobber and goodness knows what else! Even bedtime was going to be torture! Ruby and I sat in silence the whole way there while the nerds talked about their favourite Shakespeare novels - seriously! We arrived at the Lake District at lunchtime and met Miss Clay who is an outdoor bounds expert and will be coming with us on the walks. Straight away Sir was trying to act all macho. Suddenly his chest seemed to puff up and he looked like he was holding carpets under his arms - what a loser!

Well hello Miss Clay

We were shown the dormitory and my heart sank as I spotted what looked very much like a wee stained mattress. Surely prison is better than this! We got changed and had a short TWO HOUR walk! Ruby and I started to stress as tomorrow, and the next day would be at least double this!

We got back around 3pm and I already felt homesick, so I decided to phone home to say I'd arrived safely. Mom answered and thought I was in Wales, which was quite good because Dad had forgotten I was going away! I'm beginning to think they really don't care - am I really that bad! Ruby was struggling with it all - I think I may have forgotten to tell her that it was just a joke when I put on my persuasion list that we would be staying in a posh hotel!

The rest of the evening we had a lesson on map reading. Well, it may as well have been in a foreign language - I had absolutely no idea what was going on. All my effort is going to have to go into the walking - I won't have any spare to use my brain as well! Ruby's blank expression told me she was also not getting a single thing that Sir was saying.

Tuesday

Last night was a disaster. Went to bed with the stinking dog blanket and was absolutely freezing. I guess everyone else was warm in their sleeping bags as within 10 minutes I could hear at least 3 people snoring. I tried some fake coughing to wake them up, but it didn't work. Then, annoyingly, I needed the toilet. After half an hour of trying to hold it in, I gave up and forced myself out of bed with the dog blanket wrapped around me to keep warm. It was so dark and creepy, my knees were actually knocking together with fear. Then I thought I felt something dart across my foot. In my panic I rushed to Ruby's bed and tapped her on the shoulder.

She didn't wake up, so I gave her a good shake. She suddenly woke - eyes wide, and a look of sheer horror on her face. She didn't scream at first - she must have been in so much shock, but then it came! Her scream made me scream. And then suddenly, everyone else in the dormitory was screaming as I frantically tried to make it back to my bed. Eventually the screaming stopped and luckily so had the snoring. Well, that's one way to shut the snorers up! But it didn't really matter, because for the rest of the night, I lay awake with my bladder ready to pop!

The big topic of conversation at breakfast was the 'ghost' that appeared last night in the dormitory! I thought it best not to tell anyone that it was just me with the dog blanket wrapped round me. After breakfast and a quick brief on Health and Safety, we set off. First, we climbed mountain 1 and then mountain 2 - they do have proper names, but I can't remember what they are. The nerds were talking about books again, so Ruby and me went on ahead. Sir said he was pleasantly surprised we were making so much effort. We didn't tell him it was just so I could get away from the nerdy talk. We finished the walk late afternoon - just as well as I don't think my body could take much more. I'm going to fake a sprained ankle for tomorrow as I can't face going again.

Wednesday

I think someone may have used the sprained ankle trick before, because the first thing Sir said when we went down for breakfast was, 'And I don't want any of you claiming you've sprained your ankle to get out of today's walk.' Darn it!

Today was the Langdale Pikes. I googled it on my phone - 7 miles and rated as DIFFICULT! Sir put Ruby and me in charge of map reading for the first mile - we were screwed. Map reading has always been a weakness - I blame Mom as she is pretty bad too. It is the only time Mom and Dad argue - when Dad is driving and Mom is trying to navigate. Anyway, we had no idea where we were going, but there were a couple in front of us, so we decided to just follow them. Sir seemed really impressed, but I think also slightly suspicious at our amazing map reading skills. Finally, our turn was over and Ruby and me high-fived each other thinking we'd got away with it. But before someone else took over, Sir asked us where we thought we were on the map. Ooops! I pointed to the wrong side of the mountain, but this was better than Ruby as she pointed to the car park!

Thursday

What a day! In the morning, me and Ruby had the biggest falling out we've ever had - it was messy! We were up at 6 am, because it was our turn to make breakfast for everyone else. Straight away, Ruby was irritating me as she was next to useless and had no clue what to do. I could feel myself getting stressed as time ticked on and we were nowhere near ready, so we ended up arguing. I told her it was pathetic that she didn't even know how to cook an egg. She called me bossy. I then called her a spoilt brat and that Mommy and

Daddy do everything for her. Well, can you believe it? She threw an egg straight at me! It landed straight on my head! And then the real blow came,

You really are Marjorie Egghead now!!

Well, I flashed! I launched a whole box of eggs back at her, with the final one hitting her just as Sir walked through the door. He was about to let rip at us when Miss Clay appeared and he suddenly softened up. We were ordered out to go and clean ourselves up and to be back quick sharp to sort the mess out in the kitchen. I was about to leave when Sir asked for a word. He smiled as he said it, 'That was your last chance Pickering - the end of term trip is cancelled for you!'

I wasn't sure what hurt most, no Alton Towers or Ruby calling me Marjorie Egghead! I could feel the tears welling up and I tried to stop them, but they came thick and fast! Ruby was quick to apologise over and over, and we made up by the time we got back to breakfast. We cleared up and made jam on toast for everyone instead - even Ruby could manage that!

But there was more to come! The weather was terrible - it was freezing with blustery winds - but we still went ahead with the walk. I think Sir just wanted to show off to Miss Clay as he was being particularly energetic. He was obviously trying to prove how super fit he was. He kept bounding up the hill to where the nerds were and bounding back down to where me and Ruby were - at the back. But on one of his attempts to bound back up, he suddenly disappeared - he had fallen waist deep into a bog. Well, suddenly things were looking up!

Everyone else hadn't seen what happened, so had gone on ahead. Ruby and me stood next to him looking down on him and didn't say a word. There was a lot of grunting and groaning and cursing. I could see he was desperate to get out himself and asking for help would have been a sign of weakness - so we just continued to look on. After several minutes, it was pretty clear he was going further in and there was no way he would be able to get out by himself. He said it really quietly at first. I made out I couldn't hear him and asked him to repeat his plea for help - I knew this would really hurt. 'Can I please have some assistance?' A few moments later, me and Ruby managed to haul him out, but instead of being grateful, all we got was, 'Not a word you two – understand?' It was another one of those moments where the words came out of my mouth without me really thinking what I was doing. I couldn't believe I heard myself saying - ever so quietly. 'I'll try to remember not to say anything Sir, if you can fix the Alton Towers trip for me.'

'Deal,' he replied, before I'd even registered what had happened. A few moments later, I didn't need Ruby to tell me that I 'd just managed to blackmail Sir!

We eventually made it to the top of the hill where Miss Clay was waiting for us with the nerds - and a tall, dark handsome man. It was just the best seeing the look on Sir's face when he got introduced to Will - Miss Clay's rock-climbing Olympian boyfriend! He had climbed the mountain from the other side to make a surprise appearance.

By the look on Sir's face, it definitely was a surprise - the puffed-up chest was suddenly deflated along with his ego!

Back at the centre we had dinner and then got packed up ready to leave. On the coach on the way home, I felt really happy. I can't say it was because I was now going on the Alton towers trip, as that was beginning to stress me out - I'm pretty sure blackmailing a teacher is a permanent exclusion offence! It can't be the walking, as my body aches everywhere! I might have to admit that I'm looking forward to going home and seeing everyone - even David and Emily!

Tuesday

It has taken only 2 days for Emily to start annoying me again! Over the weekend, she made a deal with Mom and Dad. They offered her £30 if she was prepared to give up her disgusting, filthy, smelly blanket that she's been wiping her nose on since she was a baby. Ten minutes after the deal was done, my cunning little sister found a doll's house on-line and spent her £30. But I could see exactly what was going to happen. Doll's house ordered and there was no going back. Her first night without the blanket and the tears came. Mom and Dad came rushing in with, you can guess what - her stinking blanket - they had kept it just in case. So gross blanket back to Emily and she gets to keep the doll's house that arrives tomorrow. Honestly!

Friday

Trip day and what a day it turned out to be! Sir had stuck to the deal and I was allowed to go to Alton Towers.

I've always loved Theme Parks and the faster and scarier the ride, the better. But Ruby planted a seed of doubt in my head as we were about to get on the first ride. She told me, as people get older, they can't tolerate spinning round and round as much - they just puke! I told her not to be so ridiculous, but when I got off the first ride, I was not feeling 100% and should have had a bit of a break. But I didn't!

By ride three, I felt so ill, I was desperate to get off - I really thought I might actually die! When it eventually stopped, I didn't make a scene. I skulked off without telling anyone and found a quiet place to recover. But! As I prepared myself for the worst, I heard someone call my name. I looked up to find Smug Smithy with 2 of his mates heading straight towards me. Before I knew it, he was right in front of me laughing and making fun of me because I looked like death. I tried to warn them, but I could feel it coming and there was nothing I could do. They were about a metre away, but the projectile vomit managed to hit Smithy from the knees down.

His mates had managed to dodge it, but Smithy was in so much shock, he didn't move and had no time to dodge the second lot! In all the chaos, I couldn't help but notice that as well as the usual carrots - I'd puked up a whole sausage! Mom is right - I really do need to chew my food more!

The screams from Smithy were delayed for a few seconds, but when they came, they managed to drown out every other fun scream that was happening on the rides. I tried to apologise, but vomit 3 and 4 followed soon after. His flight mechanism luckily kicked in by this time, so he was spared any more. I managed to clean myself up and phoned Ruby to explain my disappearance. I felt dreadful, but I couldn't help smiling at the image I had of Smithy covered in my puke!

Monday

Poor Grandad was rushed into hospital yesterday because he had a heart attack. His cleaner found him collapsed on the kitchen floor surrounded by wrappers from the lucky dip. Grandad busted! Mom and Dad must be worried as they told us he is staying with us this year for a whole week of the Christmas holiday.

Saturday

Unbelievable!! Mom and Dad told us this morning that they've decided not to do Christmas presents this year after what happened last year. And I thought Scrooge and Grinch were just made up!!

I'm totally blaming David for this. Last year, about a week before Christmas, Mom and Dad went out, and David decided he was going to open the wrapped Christmas presents he'd found hidden under Mom and Dad's bed.
Anyway, stupidly, me and Emily agreed to join in and be look out. If they came back early, we could sound the alarm.

I did feel slightly guilty, but to be honest, they should have found a better hiding place! Three presents in and I could tell from David's sighs, he was not impressed. The lame hiding place matched his lame presents - a Star Wars t-shirt, 5 pairs of socks and a packet of pants!

Then -disaster! - we heard the key in the door, and then the sound of footsteps coming up the stairs. No way could we clean up in time. There was only one thing for it. The three of us made a run for it at the same time and ended up getting wedged in the door frame.

Dad was coming up the stairs and I somehow managed to wiggle out in front and made it to the bathroom, just as Dad got to the top of the stairs. It is the only room in the house with a lock on the door and I'd made it to safety. Emily was never going to get told off by Dad, but I remember thinking David would be in for it. But all I heard was a bit of mumbling, and then Dad going out the front door.

Then came the knock on the bathroom door and, 'You're so dead!' So, for the next 4 hours, I had no choice but to stay put. If I left the bathroom, it would be the 'Gob drop' punishment.

So, because of David's terrible idea, we are going to give money to charity and receive 1 secret Santa present instead. And get this - the maximum spend is £5! Everyone's name will go into a hat, and we pick out a name who we will buy a present for.

Christmas Day
This is one Christmas I won't forget in a hurry! The Secret Santa presents were rubbish, but what was worse, we nearly killed Grandad - THREE times! David was first to strike, and once again I went along with his stupid idea.

He came into my room really early in the morning and somehow convinced me that he had a great idea to cheer Grandad up, after everything he had been through. The plan was to grab a couple of party poppers from downstairs and go into his room and let them off with a big, 'Happy Christmas!' At 6:30 am, we crept into the room and could hear he was still sleeping soundly. Party poppers in hand, David counted down, then BANG! And, 'Happy Christmas Grandad!'

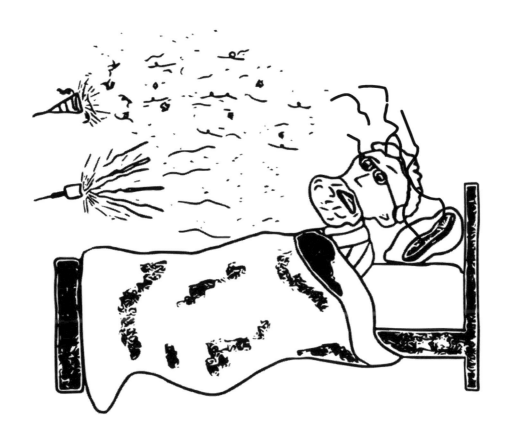

Well, I thought it was a good sign at first when he sat bolt upright, but then suddenly Grandad was clutching his chest. It was pretty clear the nice surprise hadn't really worked, and it looked like he was having another heart attack! Mom and Dad quickly appeared and took one look at our guilty faces, empty poppers in our hands and a trail of streamers draped over poor Grandad's head and didn't need to ask any questions. They were not impressed. Thinking about it now, being woken up like that is never going to be a nice surprise, let alone when you're 80 years-old and recovering from heart surgery - what were we thinking? Luckily Grandad was okay. But!

After Grandad's first dice with death, David and me were on our best behaviour and didn't dare put a foot wrong. After dinner, it was time for the 'Secret Santa.' Dad tried to pretend to be excited when he opened his potato peeler and a fishing calendar, but I could tell he wasn't happy. I was a bit disappointed that Dad didn't really like his presents - it took me ages to find such a cool potato peeler. To be fair though the calendar was free in last week's paper and was free for a reason.

David opened his present next - a box of Turkish delight - YUK! I remember seeing the same box at Grandad's house back in the summer and it was two years out of date then! Of course, I wasn't going to tell David that though. Emily got ... an iPad!! HOW IS THAT £5!

Mom was happy with a huge box of chocolates and a bottle of wine. I noticed the wine just so happened to be Dad's favourite - so no Sherlock Holmes mystery there. I was next. I opened it up and was not disappointed - it was a lovely silver pen. But I should have known better because I noticed David was looking particularly pleased with himself. I clicked the top of the pen to try it out and got a massive ELECTRIC shock!

David was laughing so much, and then everyone else joined in. And Mom and Dad wonder why I hate him so much! I ran out the lounge and went to my bedroom, determined not to go downstairs again until everyone apologised. After 20 minutes, I realised no one was coming to see if I was okay, and I could now hear they were getting ready to play charades - I love charades.
So, I went back down and joined in. All was going well until Grandad went to write down the score. He had only gone and reached for the electric shock pen without realising.

Grandad was clutching his chest again! But luckily after a few deep breaths he quickly recovered. I ended up getting the blame for not putting it in a safe place. The evening continued without any other drama and Grandad seemed to have recovered.

It was then time for bed, so what could possibly go wrong? We must have all been asleep for about an hour, when we heard an almighty scream followed by, 'It's a RAT!' coming from Grandad's room. We all arrived at the same time and flung open his door. There, sitting on top of his face was no rat, but….Hercules!!

One quick glance at us all, Hercules disappeared down the back of the bed. Poor Grandad was holding his chest once again and trying to catch his breath. Mom sat with him for the rest of the night to make sure Hercules didn't make another appearance or anything else.

Sunday - Boxing Day

So, Grandad decided this morning he wanted to cut short his stay with us and go back home. He must think we are trying to kill him off! While we were eating breakfast, Grandad announced that when he dies, he has decided that he is leaving all his money to the cat's home. Mom and Dad smiled awkwardly and agreed it was a good idea, but I noticed Dad suddenly go a bit pale. Charlie suddenly perked up though.

Nice one Grandad!

Wednesday

So, the rest of the Christmas holiday was spent packing boxes, as tomorrow we are moving to our new house. Hercules is obviously alive and well, but even with the whole house packed up, we still haven't found him. I told Dad that we should probably warn the new owners about Hercules, just in case he made another surprise appearance. But Dad's vein popped up just hearing the name Hercules, so I thought it best to leave it.

Saturday

All packed up. we left our house for the final time, but as Mom locked the door, one of the old ladies from the retirement home next door shouted from her window. 'Excuse me.'
Mom glared up, 'Yes?'
A drum roll for the response.
'Just to let you know, we've all had so much enjoyment watching your delightful children grow up over the past 10 years - we're going to miss you all.'
Now, I did not see that coming!

I'm not that bad after all!!

Printed in Great Britain
by Amazon

87689829R00066